The Intergalactic Omniglot

The Intergalactic Omniglot

Jenni Fleetwood

ORCHARD BOOKS
London

For Alexander, Nicholas and Katie

The Intergalactic Omniglot

Chapter 1

The sound was most insistent. It invaded Jamie's sleep, turning the bicycle in his dream into a screaming jet. Eventually he could ignore it no longer and sat up in bed, trying to identify the source of the high-pitched whine.

The telly. That was it. Dad must have left it on when he came to bed.

Jamie slid his legs over the side of the bunk and found his slippers. The huddled shape that was his brother Cameron did not move. The house was in darkness. Across the landing Alice was fast asleep and there were gentle snores coming from his parents' bedroom. Evidently nobody else had heard the sound. Jamie padded down the stairs, still half asleep, to turn the telly off.

It wasn't on.

Now the sound was all about him. It seemed to bounce off the walls, whirling around and around his body until he thought his head would crumple like a paper cup. He tried to call out, but could not speak.

And then, as suddenly as it had started, the sound stopped. All Jamie could hear was his own heart, clop-clopping away in his chest. He turned to run up the stairs to call his parents – and saw, through the big patio doors, the lights.

There were two of them. Different colours. The duller of the two shone with a faint blue light; the other was yellow. They appeared to hang motionless in the branches of the apple tree. And then, with a speed that made Jamie jump, they shot off in opposite directions. The yellow light made a great arc in the sky and almost disappeared from view. The blue light, which had shot upwards, seemed to hover for a moment and then it, too, shot off in the direction taken by the yellow light. It was as if one were chasing the other. Several times they sped across Jamie's vision, and then, without warning, they were gone.

Jamie shook his head from side to side. Everything was back to normal. He grabbed his anorak from its hook and quietly slid the patio doors across. The garden seemed huge and rather menacing once he moved away from the door. It had been raining and he brushed against leaves that dripped on his slippered feet. An owl hooted. It might have startled another boy but when Jamie heard the sound he relaxed. Everything was all right. This was his home, 17 Hayfields Close. It was his garden, and the owl was a familiar friend.

As if to reassure him further, the clouds parted for a moment and a full moon lit the path back to the house.

Next morning at breakfast he told the family what he had seen. He didn't mention the high-pitched sound – somehow that was more personal and he wasn't ready to share it yet.

Cameron was furious. 'Why didn't you wake me up, you mean pig!'

'Don't be ridiculous, Cameron,' said Mrs Mackenzie. 'I don't suppose Jamie had time to wake anyone – and what is more, if anybody round here is a pig it is the one stuffing his face with Honey Smacks.'

'It seems you weren't the only person to see the lights, Jamie,' said his father, looking up from his copy of the *East Anglian*. 'Look at this.'

A large headline near the bottom of page one read 'MYSTERY LIGHTS IN SUFFOLK SKY'.

'Read it to us, Angus,' said Mrs Mackenzie.

' "In the early hours of this morning, strange lights were spotted in the night sky over Suffolk. The lights were seen along a coastal strip between Slimwich and Buntisden, with most sightings reported within a five-mile radius of the town of Grantwell.

"It was at first assumed that what watchers had seen was a night exercise by helicopters or aircraft from the United States Air Force Base near Bambridge, but the Base Commander categorically denies that any such exercise took place.

"Could it be that we have been visited by UFOs?

"Mr Michael Chandler (48), whose farm is on the outskirts of Grantwell, reported seeing six lights, all radiating outwards from a central source 'Like a giant firework'." '

'Rubbish,' said Jamie, 'there were two: one blue, one yellow. I told you.'

'*You* saw two,' said his mother. 'Carry on, Angus.'

' "Mr Chandler, who saw the lights when he got up to tend a sick cow, also told us that this morning all his hens had refused to lay. Similar reports have been coming in from other parts of the county." '

'That's a good one,' said Mrs Mackenzie. 'They'll be seeing two-headed donkeys next.'

It was time for school. Jamie slung his knapsack on his back, climbed on to his old bike and pedalled off down the road, his mother's warning about being careful still singing in his ears.

Everyone was talking about the newspaper report. It seemed, however, that Jamie was the only pupil who had actually seen the lights and he had to tell his story over and over again.

At dinner time he was pulled out of the pudding queue by the headmaster, Mr Glaser, who said there was a reporter from Anglia News, the television people, who wanted to interview him. Mr Glaser said he had checked with Jamie's parents, who had no objection to Jamie talking to the Press.

It was very exciting. They asked all sorts of questions and then arranged to meet Jamie at home after school, so that they could film him in the garden.

Jamie rang his mother at work and told her.

She immediately threw a wobbler. 'Oh dear, I'll have to rush home and get the washing in. And I'd better get Ted down to cut the grass. Can you sweep the patio? Is your uniform clean?'

Jamie hung up quickly before she could think of anything else. She'd be telling him to get his hair cut next.

* * *

16

All the neighbours found jobs to do in their gardens when the television crew arrived. Jamie thought there would be loads of lights and clapperboards and make-up girls and dressers, but there was only the interviewer, a sound recordist and a single cameraman. Jamie had to stand in the garden and point out the exact spot where the lights had first appeared. At one point it was suggested he might put his pyjamas on, but thankfully that idea was overruled.

All Jamie's friends watched Anglia News that night, and Dad videoed it. Jamie thought he looked rather daft but it was fun to be a celebrity for a few days.

The national newspapers took up the story. There were lots more interviews, including one with a private pilot who said he had seen the lights too, and was certain they were nothing to do with an earthly craft. They travelled much too fast and were too manoeuvrable.

Jamie read every report avidly, searching for a reference to the high-pitched tone. It was never mentioned. Was he the only person in Suffolk to have heard it?

Chapter 2

After a couple of days the excitement began to die down. There were no more sightings and Jamie quickly found that nothing flees faster than fame. By the weekend he was being treated as a bit of a joke.

'Seen any more flying saucers, Jamie?'

'Has ET called yet?'

Mrs Mackenzie had had more than enough, too. Cranks kept pitching up on the doorstep with leaflets entitled 'Visitors from Outer Space' and articles about out-of-body experiences. A salesman tried to sell Jamie a telescope and there were a couple of men who walked right into the house without knocking and only disappeared – fast – when Mrs Mackenzie caught them looking with interest at the video recorder.

After that she locked the door.

Saturday afternoon came. Jamie's dad announced he was taking Alice and Cameron to the pictures. Mrs Mackenzie was off to a jumble sale.

'I'll stay home, Mum,' said Jamie.

'Oh, no you won't,' replied his mother. 'Not with all these strange characters about. You've got two choices. Pinocchio with Dad and the tiddlers – or the jumble sale with me.'

Jamie chose the jumble sale.

Five minutes later they pulled up outside the hall. Mrs Mackenzie (her name was Ethel but Jamie didn't call her that) joined a queue with lots of other women, some with small children, all with carrier bags, and some with push-along trolley baskets.

Jamie stood at the back with several other boys, all looking dead casual but all with eyes fixed firmly on the heavy wooden doors. Almost opening time.

Jamie loved jumble sales, though he

didn't let on to his friends. He suspected many of them felt the same way, though. There wasn't much to do in the village on wet weekends and a visit to a jumble sale was sort of like a treasure hunt. You never knew what you might find under the piles of old *Beanos* and jigsaw puzzles with missing bits. Once Jamie had found a torch with three coloured lights and a flasher for sending morse code, and another time he'd come across a hussif, a sort of cloth roll with needles and cotton inside. He almost threw it away until his grandad said it was from the war and had probably belonged to a soldier. An old radio was another find. It worked perfectly and even picked up foreign radio stations. There was junk too, plenty of it, but less now that he was getting more expert.

The secret, his mother told him, was not to mess about. Decide what looked interesting and buy it straight away. If you took too long making up your mind you might miss something else. At a couple of pence a time it didn't matter if you bought some rubbish – you could always donate it to the next jumble sale.

The doors were opening. Jamie paid his five pence to get in and headed straight for the books. Nothing much there but he picked up a couple of Roald Dahls and a copy of *The Lion, the Witch and the Wardrobe*.

He also got a book each for his little brother and sister. *One Hundred Bad Jokes* for Cameron, and a book about the Brownies for Alice. The tiddlers were always at the door when they got home and expected Jamie to bring them something. Next, a real find. An almost brand-new copy of *The Neverending Story*. He loved that book. He had borrowed it from the library and Mum had read it in the evenings. Now that he was nine he was a bit old for bedtime stories, but his mother pretended she was only reading them for Alice and Cameron's sake, so that was all right.

There was his mum now. Over by the children's clothes. She'd already filled one bag. She was a genius at jumbles. Lots of their clothes came from her Saturday afternoon sort-outs. When she got home and tipped the bags out on to the carpet, it was like

Christmas and birthdays rolled into one. There were always some peculiar things, too: huge hats with lace and flowers; see-through nighties in pink or blue; men's waistcoats and cloth caps; ballet tutus and rugby jerseys. All for the dressing-up box. The Mackenzies' dressing-up box was known throughout the town. Children who came to play with the tiddlers never bothered with toys. It was much more fun to be pirates and kings or queens.

Jamie turned back to the tables. Things were hotting up. There were heaving bodies everywhere, hands flying in the air, people pushing, shoving, barging in. And all for items which were second-hand and sold for less than ten pence.

Toys or White Elephant? Both were usually promising. Jamie decided on the White Elephant and got to the front of the crowd by the simple trick of crawling under a table and coming out just where he wanted to be. 'Sorry,' he said to the woman under whose skirt he almost emerged, 'just been picking up the records.'

He found a good buy almost immediately.

A large cassette case. Just the thing for his computer tapes. It went into the bag with the books. Then there was a sprinkler that looked as though it would work. Dad had been saying he must buy one now that the strawberry bed was established. Once the weather warmed up, if it ever did, a sprinkler would be really useful. Jamie bought it and then noticed a smallish tin box. At least, it looked like tin. What caught his eye was the design on the lid: two linked stars. Inside was a meter of some kind. Maybe one of those things to check electrical current, Jamie thought. He remembered Mum's rule. Grab first, think about it afterwards. The lady behind the counter let him have the box for a penny. She didn't know what it was either.

Time for a drink. Jamie elbowed his way to the hatch at the back of the hall. Ten pence got him a plastic cup of orange squash and two biscuits. He sat down on the row of chairs that had been placed back to back down the middle of the hall, mostly for the many pensioners waiting patiently for the draw and their weekly chance to win a bottle of sherry.

Ted Harris sat down beside him. Jamie liked Ted. He was a retired policeman who sometimes did some work in the garden. He told marvellous stories about life in the police force when he was a bobby on the beat, and what he didn't know about Grant-well wasn't worth knowing. Jamie read him some of the jokes in the book he'd bought for Cameron. The title was right. They were bad. Ted said enough was enough and moved away. His place was taken by an Indian lady in a sari. She had a friend with her, and Jamie moved up so that she could sit down. They started chatting in a language Jamie couldn't understand. He returned to his purchases. The little box was a puzzle. Maybe Mum or Dad would know what it was for. He traced the design on the lid with his finger. The two Indian women were still talking animatedly. Jamie heard one of them say she had hoped there would be plants for sale but she hadn't been able to find any.

'They're outside,' said Jamie, closing the box. 'They always have them outside because it's cooler. Things wilt in here.'

'Thank you,' said the taller of the two women, 'but please tell me, how is it that you understand Hindi? Have you lived in India?'

'I don't understand Hindi,' said Jamie, putting the little box into his pocket. 'You were talking in English.'

The woman looked puzzled. 'I speak a little English,' she said, 'but my friend is newly arrived in England and knows none. We were talking in Hindi.'

She turned to her companion and rattled off an explanation in the language Jamie had heard before. This time he couldn't understand a single word.

Chapter 3

Mrs Mackenzie plonked herself down next to Jamie. 'Great jumble,' she said happily. 'I've got no end of bargains. Did you find anything exciting?'

'Nothing much,' said Jamie, for some reason not wanting to say anything about the little box with the star pattern on the lid. 'I got a cassette case and some books for Cameron and Alice. And a sprinkler for Dad.'

'That'll be useful,' she said, examining it. 'It's a bit stiff but a drop of oil will soon put that right. Did you buy any draw tickets?'

'No.'

'Never mind. I've got two lots. You can check the green ones.'

26

She handed Jamie a strip of tickets as a short tubby man got up on the stage. After the usual speech thanking everyone for attending and for donating such wonderful prizes, he asked his wife to draw the first ticket.

'It's a blue ticket. Blue four-three-six.'

A nervous-looking woman scuttled up to the stage and scooped up the biscuit tin with the picture of Prince Charles and Princess Diana.

'A green ticket this time. Green thirty-three. An early buyer.'

It was Ted. Jamie was pleased. Ted got a bottle of whisky and a clap from his mates.

The tall Indian woman won the next prize. A clematis. Jamie hoped she had a garden. But she must have, she had asked about the plants. Funny that, thinking he had understood what they were saying. The woman must have spoken in English without realizing it.

'Now come on, ladies and gentlemen, someone must have Green two-eight-seven!'

'Jamie!' His mother shook his shoulder.

27

'It's ours. For heaven's sake stop dreaming and get up on that stage. Choose the chocolate cake.'

The tiddlers would be pleased. Chocolate cake for tea. Mrs Mackenzie almost always won a prize – she was amazingly lucky. Sometimes it was a bottle of wine or a pack of beers for Dad; once there was a beautifully dressed doll for Alice. It was supposed to say 'Mama' but the string was broken. Still, you couldn't have everything, Mum said, not from a jumble sale.

At home again Mrs Mackenzie proudly showed off her purchases: shorts for both boys, a Middle School pullover for Jamie, two dresses for Alice. There was a double bedspread and, best of all, a hammock. 'I got it for fifty pence,' said Mrs Mackenzie. It was a wonderful hammock, made of cloth, with a padded pillow and long tassels.

'I can't wait for the summer,' said Jamie's dad. 'I'll be out there between the apple trees.'

'After you set up the sprinkler,' said Jamie. And everybody laughed.

The books were very well received, but Jamie didn't show anyone the box in his pocket. He wanted to study it more closely before he mentioned it.

Much later, when Alice and Cameron were asleep, Jamie reached under his pillow and brought out the box. He examined it by the light of his tri-coloured torch. It was quite small, smaller than his calculator, and the surface was faintly pitted as though someone had thrown gravel at it while it was being moulded. In colour it was a dark red. Jamie had never seen another metal quite like it. It wasn't copper, he was sure of that. His Uncle Tom had worked on the Copperbelt in Zambia and had sent his mother loads of copper ornaments. None of them looked anything like the box.

Inside was another puzzle. The star design was repeated, but faintly, inside a circle. Around the edge of the circle were markings, sort of squiggles. They didn't look at all familiar. They weren't numbers, or at least Jamie didn't think so. There were eight of them, regularly spaced. Jamie got out his ruler. Yes, each was a precise distance from the next. In the centre of the circle was a single needle, like the minute hand on a watch. Only it didn't move. Jamie tried wiggling it about but it was solid. Rusted maybe.

Perhaps Dad could make some suggestions. Moving quietly, so as not to waken Cameron in the bunk below, Jamie slipped out of the room. Mum was out – she played darts on Saturday nights. Dad was in the lounge watching a film. It sounded like a love film. Jamie could hear a man's voice talking about a woman's body. It was very descriptive and Jamie felt himself starting to blush.

'Hey, Dad,' he called, 'that doesn't sound like your sort of film. Hot stuff, eh!'

'Oh, I'm only waiting for "Match of the Day" to start,' said his father. 'Anyway, how would you know what the film is about?'

Jamie walked into the lounge. The film had English subtitles containing a condensed and, to Jamie's mind, rather disappointing version of events on the screen.

'It's a Swedish film. Beyond me,' said Mr Mackenzie. 'Turn it off if you like.'

It was weird. How come Jamie could suddenly understand foreign languages?

'If you've come down for a drink,' said Mr Mackenzie, 'you can have a glass of milk. And bring me a beer from the fridge, please.'

Jamie got the drinks and then showed his father the box. 'Any idea what this is, Dad? I got it at the jumble.' He didn't mention the strange events of the day. Time enough for that later, if he ever worked out what was going on.

'It looks like some sort of meter.'

'That's what I thought.'

'I don't recognize the metal, nor the workmanship,' said Mr Mackenzie. 'These signs here, around the circle, they could be Chinese characters, I suppose. They look a bit like the markings on the mah-jong set.'

Jamie got the set out of its rosewood case and looked at one of the bamboo-and-ivory tiles. Yes. The signs did look a bit like Chinese characters – it was hard to tell.

'Whatever it is, it doesn't work. This

central hand seems to have seized up,' said Mr Mackenzie. 'Take it to school tomorrow. See what the teachers make of it.'

'On Monday.'

'Pardon?'

'Take it to school on Monday. It's Sunday tomorrow.'

Jamie's dad grinned. 'So it is. Well, seeing as you don't have to get up for school, why not stay down here and watch the football with me?'

It was a jolly good game. Jamie enjoyed nights like these, when there were just the two of them. During the day the tiddlers got most of the limelight. Cameron was six, Alice five, so it wasn't surprising.

It was late when Jamie got to bed. He heard his mother come in and her laughter as she told Dad about her evening. Then his parents went to bed, and the house was quiet. Jamie couldn't sleep. He reached out to the shelf above his bunk and quietly turned his radio on. Cameron wouldn't wake up now. Once he was really asleep an earthquake wouldn't shift him, but if Mum or Dad heard there would be hell to pay.

The radio was set to 'Voice of America'. Jamie liked that station. There was plenty of music, but interesting talks, too. They were playing an old Dylan number. Perhaps it would send him to sleep.

And then Jamie sat bolt upright. He twiddled the knob on the radio. Radio Moscow. Russian. Naturally he couldn't understand what was being said. But wait, every time he'd found himself able to understand a foreign language he had been holding the box. He picked it up now. Nothing. Not a flicker. Absentmindedly he fingered the design on the lid, and immediately the words coming from the radio made perfect sense. It was a very boring talk about grain production, but every word was clear.

Whatever the box was, wherever it had come from, Jamie had the feeling it was going to change his life.

Chapter 4

Jamie very nearly missed school on Monday. He had been very quiet on Sunday morning and kept disappearing to his bedroom. His mother thought he might be going down with something and blamed Mr Mackenzie for keeping him up so late on Saturday night.

She didn't know that Jamie spent every possible moment tuning to foreign radio stations, discovering every time that when he touched the star pattern on the little red box he could understand whatever was being discussed. He quickly discovered that he didn't actually have to trace the outline of the stars; just touching them lightly was enough.

Jamie couldn't wait to get to school. First period was French, his least favourite subject. He had always thought it was really unfair that they had to start the week with something he was so appallingly bad at. And with the teacher he liked least.

Old Penfold, as the boys called him, was small, busy and bald. The boys had nicknamed him after a television character but they all agreed that the cartoon Penfold was a lot more fun. For Penfold, teaching French was like working with clay in the pottery class. It was something to be pummelled, punched and slapped down on the table. He would have liked to have treated the boys the same way.

He faced them now.

'Watch out,' said Jamie's friend Robin. 'His whiskers are twitching.' Jamie giggled, which was always fatal.

'All right, Jamie, stand up. We'll see whether you find life so amusing after a spell of French translation.'

Jamie stood up. His right hand rested lightly on the desk. Under his hand was the box.

Penfold read, very rapidly, a paragraph in French. 'Now, boy, translate, if you would be so kind.'

'Yes, sir. I'll do my best, but without making notes it can only be a rough translation.'

The class hooted. This was going to be a good day. Penfold felt his anger rising, but held it down. Let the boy speak. Let him make his usual hash of things. Then Penfold could take him apart, gradually. With luck he could make the humiliation last all lesson. For Penfold it would be a good day too.

Jamie spoke quietly. 'Sir, the piece you read was taken from *Paris Match*. June last year, I think you said. It described the vineyards of Burgundy. You mentioned, I think, sir, four types of grape: Pinot Noir and Gamay, which are used for making red wines, and Chardonnay and Alliage, which are used for white wines. The grapes are not usually blended.'

Penfold was dumbstruck. The translation was almost totally correct. The boy had said Alliage when he should have said Aligote, but otherwise he hadn't put a foot wrong.

For one dazzling moment, the French teacher knew pure joy. Could it be that after all the years, all the barren years, he had suddenly started to inspire his pupils? If Jamie Mackenzie, one of his least able students, could reel off a perfect translation of such a difficult piece of writing, what standards could be reached by the rest of the class?

No. It was impossible, quite impossible. There must be some elaborate hoax here. The *Paris Match* had been in his briefcase, open at the article on wine. He'd never intended to use it in class. It was way beyond even the fourth years. No. He'd marked the article because his love of wine was the one thing that made teaching bearable. When he retired he was going to live in France and write a book about the grape.

'So, Jamie, you've suddenly become a genius, eh! Yesterday you couldn't understand directions to the station; today you read *Paris Match*. Come up to my desk, lad, and let's repeat the experiment.'

Jamie quickly pocketed the box and went to stand beside the teacher. *Monsieur* (as he liked to be called) rattled off two sentences about cheese-making, this time making them up so as to make sure the boy had not read them beforehand. His voice sounded like machine-gun fire, with Jamie the victim.

'You said, sir, that the cattle that graze on the slopes of the Alps produce excellent dairy products. These include Emmental, Reblochon and . . .'

'That's enough,' shouted Penfold, his face dark red like the box. 'If you're so clever, let me hear you say it in French. Go on, Jamie, we're all waiting!'

Jamie felt the flesh above his lips grow cold. He hadn't thought of that. The device helped him understand foreign languages but it did nothing for his tongue.

'Come on, Jamie. Spit it out.'

Jamie tried. It was hopeless. He didn't know the words. Penfold was going to have his fun after all.

'So, Jamie, the muse has deserted you. Well, let's try French to English again.'

Jamie breathed once more – until he heard Penfold's next sentence.

'And take your hands out of your pockets when you talk to me, boy. Don't you have any manners at all?'

At break time Jamie stayed in the classroom. Robin kept him company.

'Jamie! How did you do that trick this morning? We really thought you had got the better of old Penfold for once. It was brilliant. How did you know he was going to ask you for that particular bit of translation?'

'I didn't.'

'Oh, come on, Jamie. I'm the one whose homework you copy, remember. You didn't understand all that stuff.'

Suddenly Jamie felt furious with himself. He'd thought he was so clever, bringing the box to school. He was going to make Penfold look such a fool. And he had nearly succeeded. So nearly. He'd just forgotten the important fact that understanding isn't much use without communication. The device didn't look like being much use to him after all.

'Okay, Rob, I'll tell you, but only if you

give me a hand with those five pages of translation Penfold socked me with.'

'Right.'

Jamie told him the whole story; about the jumble and the Indian women and the Swedish film and the radio stations.

'I don't believe it.'

'I'm not sure I believe it myself. But it's true. Here's the box.'

Robin held the box carefully, as if afraid it might suddenly catch fire. Like Jamie, and Jamie's dad, he tried to shift the hand in the centre of the circle, but failed.

'Prove it works, Jamie. Just for me.'

'How am I supposed to do that?'

'The translation!'

'That's no good. It only works on sounds, not the written word.'

Robin stood up. 'I know that, idiot, but don't you see, I can read the French. My accent's not fantastic, but it's not bad. Then you can write down the English. It'll save hours – if it works.'

It worked.

Robin was impressed. 'It's fantastic. Where do you suppose it was made?'

'China, my dad thinks. I'm not sure.'

'Let me borrow it, please, just for one night!' Robin wheedled. 'I'll give you ten football stickers.'

It was a tempting offer. Ten stickers might just give Jamie the last member of the Arsenal team.

'Okay, but just for one night. And don't try to be clever with it. If anyone else finds out about this I'll never speak to you again.'

Chapter 5

'It didn't work.'

Robin was standing outside the school gate, looking very disappointed.

'What do you mean?'

'What I said. I copied you exactly, putting my fingers on the design on the lid and nothing happened, not a thing. I tried it with a German radio station, then a Dutch one. I even tried it on my old gran. She's Polish and I asked her to say something. I couldn't understand a word of it.'

'That was taking a chance.'

'No. Not really. I had the box in my pocket all the time. She didn't suspect anything. Why should she? I often ask her to talk in Polish.'

Jamie took the box and slipped it into his anorak.

'Do you suppose the batteries have run down?'

'Could be. How can you tell? One thing's for sure – they don't sell replacements at the supermarket!'

Robin was reluctant to part with the football stickers but they finally agreed on five. The Arsenal goalkeeper wasn't among them.

After school, Jamie and Cameron had a swimming lesson at the baths in Bambridge.

Bambridge is a pretty little town, about fifteen miles from Grantwell. It was a beautiful drive along the sleepy little Suffolk lanes, now just beginning to come to life after the hibernation of winter. The first snowdrops huddled together under the budding oak and ash trees. Soon the daffodils would be out, their bright banners a sign that the sun would shine again.

Their route took them past the American airbase, with its long, low buildings and modern un-English shopping complex. Jamie loved going to the Base. He didn't often get the chance, for it was off-limits to all but the people who worked there, but sometimes one of his American friends would invite him to go bowling or to have a hamburger at the club. The burgers were great, big and meaty and covered in relish. Once you had tasted one you never wanted a Wimpy again.

They stopped to watch an A-10 coming in to land. It was an ungainly-looking aeroplane. Cameron loved them but Jamie preferred the sleeker F-16s that his friend Adam's father flew.

The stop made them a bit late and both boys tore into the swimming pool, glad they had put their costumes on under their tracksuits. It was always better when Mum took them swimming. Dad insisted upon coming into the changing room with them to make sure they took a shower after the lesson. The showers were icy and only the supervised used them.

'And now,' said Mrs Mackenzie, when they joined her and Alice in the car, 'what do you say to the Greek?'

'Yes, please!'

Grantwell's Greek restaurant came as a surprise to visitors. Sandwiched defiantly between the chippie and the newsagents, it looked rather too exotic for such a small country town, like a guava at the greengrocers. Local people shook their heads when it opened and at first continued to eat, when they ate out at all, at the pub on the corner where you could be sure of plaice and chips or steak-and-kidney pie. But Andreas' looked inviting, with its hand-painted murals, its simple scrubbed tables and bazouki music. It was cheap, too, and they served marvellous pizzas as well as traditional Greek food.

Mrs Mackenzie loved it. She and Angus had been among its first customers, and on Tuesdays, swimming-lesson days, Dad always met them at their usual table beside the fish tank.

'Hello, love, had a good day?'

'Pretty fair. And you?'

The parents were off. None of the children would get a word in for a while. Cameron and Alice went to watch the fish. They played a game where each chose a fish and the one whose fish came up for air first was the winner.

Jamie took off his anorak and hung it on the back of his chair. As he did so, something fell out of his pocket and on to the floor.

'What was that, Jamie?' asked his father.

'Nothing. Just my football stickers.'

He snatched up the box, and, under cover of the tablecloth, checked it was all right. It wasn't. Something had happened to the design on the lid. It was slightly off-centre. If Jamie hadn't looked at it so often over the past few days he probably wouldn't have noticed. Gently he prodded it and part of the box slid back smoothly, revealing a small compartment.

Carefully he slipped the box into his tracksuit pocket. 'Just going to the toilet.'

In the Gents Jamie examined the compartment more carefully. There were two indentations in it, and resting in each was a small cylindrical object, rather like a capsule. At first Jamie didn't know what they

were, and then it struck him. Earplugs! He
carefully slid them into his ears. They fitted
perfectly. He looked in the mirror. No, you
couldn't see them. He wondered if they
would affect his hearing, and turned the tap
on. He could still hear the water gurgling
into the basin, so what on earth could the
peculiar plugs be for? When he returned to
the table Mum and Dad were tucking into
their *meze*. Each had a plate containing
several different items. The pink stuff,
Jamie knew, was taramasalata, a pâté
made from cod's roe. He didn't care for it
much.

The tsatsiki was okay, if you liked cucum-
ber and yogurt, and Jamie was partial to the
calamari – until his mother told him it was
fried squid. There were olives, too, and
anchovies, and chunks of cheese. His
mother offered Jamie a bit but he declined.

'I'm waiting for my pizza, thanks.'

Johnny was a fine cook. He made the best
pizzas in East Anglia, Jamie thought,
maybe the best in England. The crust was
just the right thickness, the topping rich
and cheesy. Jamie was glad he was old

enough to have a whole one; Cameron and Alice had to share.

'Pop over and ask Johnny for some more pitta bread, please, dear,' said Mrs Mackenzie. Jamie walked over to the glass-fronted counter where Johnny and his assistant Milo were chatting.

The box was in Jamie's pocket. He could feel it bumping against his leg as he walked. Was Robin right about it being broken? Maybe the fall had jolted it and it still worked. Or perhaps – and this thought hadn't occurred to Jamie before – perhaps he was the only person who could use it.

This was as good a time as any to find out. Johnny and Milo were speaking Greek, as usual. And, hurrah, Jamie could understand them. They were having a fine old gossip, discussing the customers.

'I see Mr Dibson has come in as usual,' said Johnny.

'Yes. And as usual he's getting drunk and starting to shout at his poor little wife.'

'Nice to see the Mackenzies. I'm glad they always take the table at the back of the restaurant.'

'Why?'

'So I can watch her wiggle as she walks past.'

Both men laughed. Jamie couldn't help joining in. But the words that came unbidden to his lips were not English. In perfect Greek, and very quietly, he said: 'Thank you. I've never really noticed my mother's wiggle, but I'll look out for it now!'

Johnny's face grew as red as the tomatoes on the pizza he was topping.

'You speak Greek!'

'Only a little. I've been learning in secret. So I'll make a pact with you. You don't tell my parents I can speak Greek and I won't tell them about the wiggle.'

All three of them laughed again and Jamie collected the pitta bread for his mother.

Jamie ate his pizza almost mechanically, for once hardly noticing the delicious ham-and-mushroom topping. He'd cracked it! He could understand and speak foreign languages now. The earplugs were magic. They seemed to operate only when needed. The rest of the time he could hear normally. He could hardly wait to tell Robin.

But telling Robin was the furthest thing from his mind next morning. Something was to happen in the middle of the night that was even more exciting.

Chapter 6

Jamie felt as though he had been awake for hours. Thoughts were running round and round in his head like pedals on a bicycle. What exactly was the device he had found? Who had made it? And what was it doing in a jumble sale in a village in England? Should he tell his parents about it?

That was one he could answer. No. Maybe if he had said something in the beginning – but not now. Not when he was getting better marks at French. He'd just be made to look a fool. And besides, the little box was special. He didn't want grown-ups exclaiming over it and examining it and making it theirs.

Jamie shivered. It was very cold.

Sometimes when he couldn't sleep one of his parents would make him a warm drink. But Mum was asleep and so was Dad. The house was still and silent.

It was no use. Sleep wouldn't come. He'd make himself a hot chocolate. It would only take a moment in the microwave. And maybe walking downstairs would break the spell, like when you wake during a nightmare and want to stop yourself going back into it again.

He was halfway to the kitchen when the sound came. A familiar sound. It didn't startle him. It was as if somewhere in his mind he had known that it would come and that was why he had stayed awake.

There were no lights in the sky. Not even stars. Just a faint haze where the full moon tried to penetrate the banks of cloud. But the sound was clear enough. Not loud, but very high-pitched.

Jamie opened the front door. The sound was louder than it had been inside the house, but the cold was something else. It sucked at him like a living thing. Jamie tried to close the door but could not. He needed a coat but was unable to get one. He had to go into the garden. Something was forcing him. Something that made a high-pitched noise and carried with it ice-laden air.

Jamie stood on the path, looking up. Nothing had changed but he could feel – sense – something above his head. Something evil. Above the clouds. Waiting. Drawing slowly closer.

And then for one brief second the clouds broke. Jamie was aware of a huge black shadow and then a bright light screamed across his vision, very low and so fast that Jamie could not follow its path. There was a loud boom – and all the windows in the front of the house blew in. It broke the spell. Jamie screamed. There was a rush of footsteps and his parents' voices, all jumbled together.

'Jamie. Where are you? Jamie!'

'I'm here. In the front. Something happened to the windows. Are you all okay?'

'Yes. Luckily most of the glass fell near the walls and our duvets protected us from flying bits. What were you doing in the garden at this time of night?'

Jamie was saved from having to answer by Mr Parsons from next door, pyjama-clad and wellie-booted, muttering about idiot pilots who broke the sound barrier and made all the windows blow in. He announced he was going to phone the police and stomped off again.

'Don't try to come indoors, Jamie. There's glass in the hall. Dad will bring you some boots in a minute.'

Jamie waited. He could see the top half of his father bending and straightening, bending and straightening. He must be sweeping up. Mum was in Alice's room. Both the tiddlers were crying, partly from fright and partly from the cold that was coming through the holes where the windows had been. Ordinary cold.

Half afraid still, Jamie scanned the sky. No dark shapes or bright lights hung there. It had clouded over again and there was a sudden thunderclap and then a flash of lightning. A storm must be on its way.

Jamie shivered. He shouted up to his father. 'Could you buck up with those boots,

Dad? It's cold out here and I think it's going to rain.'

'Coming!'

His father clattered down the stairs and Jamie could hear a crunching sound as he crossed to the front door.

'Here are your boots. Come on in.'

They were about to go back into the house when the police arrived. Two of them. They came into the house and stood in the kitchen, which was relatively untouched, while Jamie told his story.

He said he had heard a strange sound, had gone into the garden to investigate and had heard a loud boom. 'And then all the windows blew in.'

Everybody told Jamie what a fool he had been to go into the garden late at night, and how lucky it was that he hadn't been opening the front door when the glass panel smashed – he could have been cut to ribbons by the flying glass. But nobody questioned his story.

Everything indicated there had been a sonic boom, the sound that occurs when an aircraft crosses the sound barrier, but nobody, not the Civil Aviation Authority or the military, could cast any light upon the plane that had set up the shock wave and broken the glass. Nor could anyone explain why the zone of damage was so narrow. Only two houses were involved. The rest of the street was untouched. One thing was certain. There would be no more sleep in the Mackenzie house that night. Mum phoned Granny and Grandad, in the next village, and it was arranged that the whole family would stay there until the house could be fixed. Meanwhile the police would stand guard.

Granny and Grandad had made up the beds by the time the Mackenzies arrived. It was wonderful to be able to snuggle down to sleep at last. The storm hadn't materialized. How odd, thought Jamie, that he had heard the thunder before he had seen the lightning. Usually it was the other way around. But the thought couldn't hold him, and he slid gratefully into sleep.

Chapter 7

They stayed at Granny and Grandad's house for almost a week, while the windows were mended and the house cleaned (more or less, though they still found shards of glass for ages afterwards) and reporters came and went from Hayfields Close. One, more diligent than the rest, tracked Jamie down and tried to get an interview, but Mrs Mackenzie told the man that Jamie had slept through everything except the breaking glass, as they all had. Perhaps that was true, in a way. When Jamie thought back to that night, the cold and the terror seemed part of a nightmare. That black menace in the sky – was it just a dark cloud he had imagined to be sinister?

He hadn't dreamed up the sound, though. He was sure of that. But what sort of sound is audible to only one person? Was it something to do with the box?

Maybe it would be better to put it away for a time, at least until all the fuss had died down. When Robin asked about the box, Jamie said he hadn't been able to fix it. He couldn't resist using it to listen to foreign radio stations, though, but always late at night when Cameron was asleep.

And although he no longer took the box to school, his French did start to improve. It must be the effect of listening to so many French programmes. Whatever the reason, Jamie was glad of it. He was no longer the butt of all Penfold's so-called wit.

Things might have gone on quietly for ages had it not been for a chance encounter between Angus Mackenzie and one of his colleagues.

'I heard a strange tale at the office today.'

'Oh?'

'I was chatting to Alf Stebbings over

lunch. You know Alf. He works in the Spares Department.'

'I know him. Do go on!' Mrs Mackenzie couldn't stand it when her husband spun out a story.

'Well, Alf's brother Simon is a forester over Cranford way. Yesterday afternoon he was marking some trees for thinning when he suddenly came upon a clearing in the forest.'

Mr Mackenzie paused.

'So? There are lots of clearings in the forest.'

'Not new ones. Not clearings that appear within a week. Simon had been in that area the previous Friday, and there was a stand of pine trees there then. Now they have all simply disappeared.'

Jamie joined in. 'Were the tree stumps still there?'

'No. But Simon dug down and found the roots. All the trees appear to have been cut off at ground level and carted away. It's weird.'

'Do you think it may have been thieves?'

'Seems unlikely. First of all, why should

thieves take just those trees, and second, any operation like that would take quite a time and make a hell of a lot of noise. Somebody would have heard something. Cranford Lodge isn't far away.'

'Did anyone up at the Lodge hear anything?'

'It seems not. Lord Cranford is away at his Scottish estate at the moment and the only unusual thing the caretaker can remember was seeing those lights that made Jamie so famous. There was a loud bang close by, but he put it down to thunder.'

A loud bang. Thunder. Jamie felt that this should mean something to him. There was a vague memory, but he couldn't track it down and his father was speaking again. 'There was something else odd, too, in the clearing. All the soil was scorched, as if there had been a fire. Simon said it looked like a lightning strike, but the area involved was too great.'

'What is Simon doing about it?'

'He has to make a report, of course. Trees are valuable. He is going to see his boss tomorrow.'

'Dad!' Jamie was jumping up and down in

excitement. 'Could we go and have a look at it? Now? It's a beautiful evening for a walk.'

'Why not,' said Mum, 'we could all do with a walk before tea. Come on. It'll be an adventure.'

'I'm not sure. It is Forestry land.'

'There's a public right of way through the forest, Angus. Oh, come on, please. You so seldom get home early from work.'

Dad stood up. 'Come on then. But it'll have to be a quick walk. It'll be dark by seven.'

Cranford Forest lay to the south of Grant-well. It was a lovely spot, popular with pic-nickers and campers. The Mackenzie family knew it well. As keen birdwatchers they often walked its leafy paths.

'Where exactly is the clearing?' asked Jamie.

'Near Tolly's Hollow. You remember, where we saw that willow warbler last summer.'

They parked the car near Cranford Lodge and were soon in Tolly's Hollow, a sheltered patch filled with daffodils. It was glorious. They spread out then, Angus and Alice going in one direction, Mum and the boys in another. It didn't take long to find the clearing.

It was quite large, about the size of the Mackenzies' front garden, and perfectly symmetrical. It was also very quiet. There was no vegetation on the neatly charred forest floor, no pine needles to crackle underfoot, no birdsong. Jamie and his father paced it out. They also found the place where Simon had dug down and exposed the roots of one of the pine trees. They were fascinated and so was Mum. Alice wandered among the trees that circled the clearing, collecting pocketfuls of cones.

The blue started to leech out of the sky. Soon it would start to get dark.

'Come on, everyone,' called Mum, 'time we were off.'

'Where's Cameron?'

Jamie knew a moment of terrible fear, and then heard his brother's voice.

'Help!'

The voice came from halfway up an unusually tall pine that grew at the edge of the clearing, a lucky pine that had survived when all its neighbours had been felled.

'Come down this instant, Cameron!'

'I can't.'

'That child is going to finish me, one of these days! Go on up after him, Jamie, there's a love. Talk him down.'

It wasn't the first time Cameron had got stuck up a tree. He was always doing it. Like Tigger he found the going up easy; it was just the coming down he didn't like.

Jamie shinned up the tree. It was easy; there were lots of branches for footholds. Cameron was grinning at him. Jamie had the feeling he could easily have climbed down on his own.

'Come on, Cameron, down we go.'

Cameron started to climb down. Jamie watched him go and then looked at the clearing, now an eerie sight in the gathering gloom.

He looked. And looked again. The burned area had shades of dark and light not visible from the ground. They formed a pattern. A pattern Jamie recognized. It was the design on the box.

Chapter 8

A week later Cranford Forest was closed to the public. The official story was that a rare bird was nesting somewhere in its midst, and rather than disclose the exact location and risk alerting thieves in search of eggs, the Forestry Commission (in consultation with the RSPB) had decided to restrict access until further notice.

Jamie told nobody about the markings in the clearing. He was beginning to feel scared. It was as if someone, or something, was leaving messages for his eyes only. But what did it all mean and how was the little red box mixed up in it? Certainly it couldn't be coincidence, the similarity between the pattern on the scorched earth and the design on the lid. Or was his imagination playing tricks again? After all, Jamie reasoned, it was dusk and shadows could be deceptive. If only he had been able to take a photograph.

There was certainly no question of going back to take a second look. He cycled past the road to the Lodge one afternoon and found every break in the fencing securely guarded. The RSPB must be delighted with the protection their bird was receiving.

Half-term came and went. The Mackenzies camped in France. It was a wonderful holiday. The campsite was relatively empty and an unseasonable spell of warm weather meant they could spend part of every day on the beach.

Jamie took the box, and the earplugs, and discovered the delight of feeling he was a native in a foreign country. His own French was quite good now, though just how good he didn't let on to his parents in case they started asking awkward questions.

His parents let him do the shopping, and sometimes allowed him to go with a group of French campers to the nearby village of Rille. There he would lose himself in the market crowds, listening to the bustle and hubbub all around him, catching a sentence here, a joke there, until he felt his head was filled with words.

His French, on these occasions, was perfect, thanks to the earplugs. The stallholders assumed he was a local boy, so the device must make him capable not only of speaking the language but of reproducing local accents. If only he understood how it worked!

He came back to the campsite after these expeditions bursting with local lore. After a couple of days he knew all about the history of the area, the gossip about the local Prefect, where to go and what to see. Mr and Mrs Mackenzie were thrilled at the extent of his knowledge. They assumed he'd palled up with one of the local French boys, many of whom spoke good English. Jamie did not disillusion them.

By the time they returned to Grantwell, Jamie felt relaxed and happy. He packed the little red box away with the souvenirs of his holiday. It had served him well, but somehow he didn't want to use it too often in England. It was time to forget the mysterious events of the past few months.

But the box wasn't finished with him yet. Twice during the next five weeks he saw the lights in the sky; first on 26 May and again on the longest day of the year, 21 June. Each time he was woken by the high-pitched hum. Each time he walked into the garden and watched in wonder. But he saw only the blue light. There was no frantic chase as in the first sighting. Instead the blue light methodically swept the heavens: north, east, south, west, dividing the sky into neat squares. Almost, Jamie thought, as if it were searching for something.

Jamie said nothing about the sightings. Nor did anybody else. There was nothing in any of the papers, no visit from excited reporters, no rumour in the town. It was as if the lights were meant for Jamie and him alone.

Curiously enough, the spectacle no longer frightened him. The light seemed harmless enough, and if it wanted to play noughts and crosses in the sky, that was its look out. Jamie's mind was filled with other things: sports day, the school outing to Pleasurewood Hills, parents' evening (for once anticipated with glee because his improved French had raised his grades) and the longed-for summer holidays.

The first event of the holidays, and the one which both Jamie and Robin looked forward to most, was the Cub camp in Cranford Forest. The forest had been reopened to the public early in June and later that month the Mackenzies had returned to the scarred clearing. But it was scarred no longer. The roots of the pines had been removed and a stand of young saplings stood where they had been. There were ferns on the forest floor, and bracken. The clearing was now just another part of the forest, and had it not been for the unmistakable shape of the tall pine Cameron had climbed, they might never have recognized it at all. Someone, said Mr Mackenzie, had gone to an awful lot of trouble.

They had picnicked in Tolly's Hollow and Cameron and Alice had persuaded Jamie to join them in a game of Packed Sardines. Alice had found an ace place to hide in a hollow tree big enough to take all three children. Remembering the tree, Jamie hoped he would have a chance to show it to Robin during the camp.

He was to get his wish – but in circumstances he would never have chosen.

Chapter 9

'Now, are you sure you've got everything?'
Jamie's mother stood in the hall, one of her
famous lists in her hand. 'Sleeping bag, pillow, blanket . . .'

'I won't need a blanket, Mum.'

'You take it. It can get very chilly
towards dawn, especially when there's
nothing between you and the earth but a
sleeping bag and a groundsheet.' Mrs
Mackenzie continued her recitation:
'Clothes, toilet bag, towel, torch, binoculars, bird book, notebook, pen, knife, fork,
spoon, mug and plate.'

'Have you put my name on?'

'Of course. See?'

'Oh, Mum! Not in pink!'

'The only thing I could find to mark this enamel was nail polish and I don't go in for green nail polish. You can say it was red but it faded.'

The one item that wasn't on Mrs Mackenzie's list was the small red box Jamie had slipped into the trouser pocket of his tracksuit. He didn't particularly want to take it with him, but he sure wasn't leaving it at home for Alice or Cameron to find.

It was an excited group of boys that gathered at the Cub hut that afternoon, each eyeing the others' bundles. Everyone seemed to have a blanket, thank goodness. One mother had actually made her son bring an inflatable airbed but was told firmly he wouldn't be needing it.

The tents had already been put up when the little minibus pulled in at the campsite, and the first thing the troop did was to set up a temporary flagpole and hoist the Union flag.

Tea was a sausage sizzle around the campfire. Jamie's sausage fell on the coals, as did many of the others, but luckily there were lots of spares. After the chores there was a quiz, and then they all sang songs until the last of the light had dimmed from the sky and it was time for bed. The Cubs slept in sixes, which meant Jamie and Robin were in the same tent. They meant to go straight to sleep, but David Ross started telling jokes, and then Allister put a rubber spider in Robin's sleeping bag and they all got a fit of the giggles.

Finally even Akela's patience was exhausted. 'The next Cub to make a sound, and I mean any sort of sound, goes home tomorrow. Have you all got that?'

They'd got it. Ten minutes later every boy in the camp was asleep.

When Jamie woke up, just after midnight, and heard the insistent high-pitched hum that was by now so familiar, his first instinct was to ignore it. He snuggled down in his sleeping bag and tried to go back to sleep. But the sound invaded the bag. It was all around him, a summons he could not ignore.

Through the open tent flap he could see the moon, fat and round and yellow, riding just above the trees. Full moon. There had been a full moon last time he'd heard the sound – and the time before that.

Jamie wriggled out of his sleeping bag and pulled on his tracksuit.

'Robin!'

The whisper sounded very loud in the comfortable silence of the tent.

Jamie dug Robin in the ribs. A sleepy head emerged, tortoise-like, from the bag. Jamie didn't give his friend time to speak. He pointed to himself, placed one finger to his lips to show they must be quiet, and slipped out of the tent with the torch in his hand.

Robin didn't need a second invitation and soon both boys were gliding quietly away from the campsite.

When it was safe to speak, Robin said crossly: 'What's going on? What did you get me up for?'

'That,' said Jamie, pointing to the north. A strange blue light hovered in the sky above the forest. As the two boys watched it seemed to grow brighter and brighter until everything – trees, tents and trails

– was washed in its unearthly radiance.

'What do you think it is?'

'I think,' said Jamie, 'that it is a space-ship. And I think it's going to land in Tolly's Hollow. Come on!'

Jamie raced off. For one sensible moment Robin thought of waking Akela, but then nosiness got the better of him, and after a few steps both boys were drawn by something more powerful than mere curiosity – a force that pulled them deeper and deeper into the forest.

Robin reached Tolly's Hollow just behind Jamie. But Jamie wasn't there. The clearing was empty in the pale blue light.

'Here.'

Jamie's voice seemed to be coming from a patch of deep shade. And then Jamie himself appeared.

'Hurry! There's a hollow tree here. We can hide in it.'

They were only just in time. Lightning had struck the old tree some time in the past and part of it was open to the sky. Looking up, the boys were almost blinded by the intensity of the light. And then, as if a shutter had come down, it was blotted out as a dark shape dropped swiftly and silently into the hollow.

Jamie almost laughed out loud. The object was a flying saucer. Not a sleek, cigar-shaped craft, not a police box, not an extraterrestrial triangle, but a comic-book flying saucer, complete with domed top and portholes around the sides. Flickers of blue flame chased each other round its under-belly and then died. There was a marking of some kind on the side – a square within a square within a square. It looked like a huge toy and for a second Jamie wondered if it were all some monstrous trick. Maybe a door would open and a game-show host would come out.

Until this moment neither boy had been really frightened. Excited, yes. Apprehensive certainly. But not scared. Too much had been happening for that. It was an adventure, that's all. Until the door did open and the creature appeared. And then they knew, for the first time in their lives, what it felt like to be terrified.

It stood upright, like a man. And, like a

man, it had two legs. Or what Jamie supposed were legs – two short stumps that supported a squat, barrel-shaped body. Four arms. Two small ones, near the centre of what, on a man, would have been a chest. Two longer arms, each one ending, like the limbs on the chest, in what looked like a mouth, a toothless clamping mouth. There was no neck. The head, if it was a head, was without any feature save for a square opening, within a square, within a square. The torso, which at first glowed a faint blue, was rapidly being covered with what looked like a creeping grey slime. Other changes were taking place, too. The legs, which had first seemed fairly stubby, were getting longer. The creature raised one of the little arms. And raised it. And raised it. The arm grew, until it brushed the marking on the side of the spaceship as if for reassurance, or perhaps as a signal. Then, as quickly as it had grown, the arm shrank. Jamie saw then that the limbs were all made up of numerous joints, apparently able to telescope into one another.

It must have been a signal, for now the

creature was joined by two more; all three flexing those horrible limbs and sweating slime.

There was a smell in the hollow now. A dank, dead smell. Jamie had never smelled anything like it before and hoped he never would again. There was sound, too. A dull sort of murmur, all on one note, or so it seemed.

Jamie became aware of Robin standing beside him, his terror matching Jamie's own. Rob, his mate. Robin, who had been his friend ever since the day when Jamie arrived at the Middle School to be teased because he was younger and smaller than all the other boys. Good old Robin. How could he have got him into this? What were the slimebags up to? That sound – was it speech? If only Jamie could find out.

But he could! Of course he could! He had the box in his pocket. He didn't bother with the earplugs – there was no way he was going to hold a conversation with the creatures – but he did slip his hand gently into his pocket until he was able to finger the design on the lid of the box.

Chapter 10

The slimebag that had emerged first seemed to be doing most of the talking. Jamie only recognized him because he was standing in front of the other two – you couldn't identify creatures by their height when they went up and down like yoyos.

'While we acclimatize, let me review the facts as we know them. The Bdrl have invented a device capable of giving every creature able to speak the opportunity of understanding and conversing with his neighbour. They call it the intergalactic omniglot. If such a device were ever to become freely available in the Murr galaxy it would spell disaster for us.'

The slimebag paused, extending one of its

lower limbs to touch the square on top of its body. It made some sort of adjustment and then continued: 'The interplanetary war that has been raging in Murr for the past thirty meganni depends upon the citizens of the nine planets continuing to distrust, misunderstand and hate one another.

'The war must go on. We, the Fwe, the finest weapon-makers since the formation of First Cell, made the war. We did not start it. We did not have to. We just sowed the seeds. Others watered them. And we gathered the harvest.' He laughed, if that choking sound was a laugh.

'And what a harvest! Who makes the instruments of war? We do. Every gun, every missile, every laser, every particle accelerator.'

Another of the slimebags spoke, but Jamie could not catch the words.

'You didn't realize, eh! Well, you youngsters don't know everything. We use many names, many faces. It would not do for our enemies to realize that their petty squabbles make us rich.'

That laugh again.

'The war *must* continue. For the first time there is a very real threat of peace. The Bdrl have actually managed to persuade representatives of all the nine planets to get together to talk about ending hostilities. I warned our leaders this might happen. As soon as the young Bdrl started spouting peace I said we should start some fresh skirmishes, give them something else to think about. Now look what could happen!

'We've grown complacent. Lazy. We take chances. We've sold identical weapons to several planets. Identical! The Bdrl plan to introduce their new toy at the conference so that delegates can communicate freely. What if they start comparing notes?'

Slime dripped from the creature's barrel body. It hissed faintly as it dropped on to the forest floor.

'The omniglot must not be allowed to appear at that conference. Not without a few modifications. A little jamming device, maybe. One we can operate at will so that only part of each conversation will be understood. Each delegate will think the others are deliberately trying to mislead him. It

80

will not be difficult to break down that fragile web of peace and goodwill, once we have studied the omniglot and provided the antidote.'

This time Jamie could hear the words spoken by the second slimebag. 'But we haven't been able to find the omniglot.'

'Not yet. But we will. We still have two lunars before the conference. We know there is only one omniglot at the moment, the prototype. It was brought here, to this sector of this planet, for testing. Bez only knows why. It's a bezforsaken little orb.'

The slimebag stopped speaking and Jamie stole a glance at the boy who stood beside him in the shadows of the hollow tree. Robin was staring fixedly at the extraterrestrials, his eyes wide, his body rigid. Jamie touched his arm, very gently, and Robin jumped. It was such a little sound, muffled by leaf mould, but to both boys it sounded like an avalanche.

The slimebags stopped their endless rise and fall. Their limbs resumed the proportions they had had when they first emerged from the spaceship. The squares on their heads darkened. And then, as Jamie and Robin watched in fearful fascination, they started to move forward. In unison. Across the clearing towards the tree. And then, very calmly, as though there was no hurry, no hurry at all, one of them extended an arm. It slithered its way over the earth. It was heading straight for Robin.

He couldn't help it. He screamed. And in that moment Jamie snapped out of the trance he had been in ever since that snakelike limb began its journey. No longer concerned about how much noise he made, he pulled the little red box out of his pocket and stuffed it into a crevice in the wooden wall behind him.

Robin had passed out. The creature had him by the ankle. It would be Jamie's turn next. He felt the hairs on his top lip grow cold. And then the welcome blackness that had engulfed Robin swept over him too, and he lost consciousness.

Chapter 11

When Jamie came to, he was lying face down in the clearing. It was dark. He turned his head very slowly to the right, expecting at any moment to feel the cold, clammy touch of the slimebag. It did not come. He risked opening his eyes. Tolly's Hollow was empty. Empty! Where was Robin? And then he saw the huddled shape in the shadows. It was Robin. He was very still. What had those creatures done to him? Jamie crawled over to where Robin sat, or rather slumped, against a tree.

'Robin, it's me, Jamie. They've gone, Rob. Oh, please be all right. Please!'

Robin said nothing. His eyes were open, staring straight ahead. He gave no sign

that he had heard or seen Jamie. Jamie
didn't know what to do. Frantic, he put his
arms around Robin's shoulders. 'Robin!
Listen to me. You are all right. We're both
all right. There's nothing here to harm you.
Stand up, Robin. Stand up!'

To his amazement Robin did stand up.

'We've got to get away from here, Robin.
Back to camp. Walk with me. Walk along
with me.'

In his anxiety over his friend, Jamie had
forgotten his own terror. Now it started to
rise again, threatening to swamp him. All he
wanted to do was run, but he couldn't leave
Robin behind. Quickly he seized Robin's
arm.

'Come on, Rob.'

Jamie had no way of knowing whether he
was getting through to his friend. Robin
walked mechanically, like a robot. They left
the clearing and passed the stand of young
pines that marked the spot where Jamie had
seen the charred earth. Jamie gripped his
friend's arm, more for his own reassurance
than anything else, and Robin shuddered, a
deep, terrible tremor that seemed to shake

his whole body. Then, for the first time, he looked at Jamie with recognition. 'Jamie. Oh, Jamie. That was horrible!'

'I know. I know. And it was much worse for you, because you didn't have any idea what it was all about. I'm sorry, Rob, it was all my fault. I should never have made you come with me.'

'Those things – were they really creatures from outer space?' Robin shuddered again, and Jamie tightened his grip on his friend's arm.

'Yes. But don't ask any more questions just now. Let's just keep walking and I'll tell you what I know.'

They walked. And Jamie talked. Using a quiet, even voice, the sort of voice his mother kept for dangerous situations, he told Robin all about the lights and the strange sound that went with them. Robin remembered the box, and grinned when Jamie told of how he had used it on holiday. He flinched when Jamie got to the bit about the slimebags, and for a moment Jamie feared his friend might be going to descend into terror again, but Robin quickly became

85

absorbed in the fantastic story.

'So the slimebags (or the Fwe, as they call themselves) didn't know you had the object they were looking for. Why didn't they find it on you?'

'I hid it. Just before they came for us.'

'Do the others know you've got it – the Bdrl?'

'I don't think so.'

'But you've got to find them, Jamie. If the Bdrl can't present the omniglot at the conference, without a Fwe jamming device, there may never be peace in Murr.'

Jamie noticed that Robin said 'you' and not 'we'. Presumably he'd had quite enough adventures with intergalactic travellers for the time being.

Something was still puzzling Jamie, though he did not like to discuss it with his friend. Why had the slimebags gone off and left them? They didn't appear to be harmed in any way. Surely beings who would happily wipe out whole planets wouldn't hesitate to kill two defenceless boys?

For answer, two lights appeared in the night sky over Orford way. For a second they seemed to hang suspended, one blue, one yellow. And then the blue light shot off, the yellow in pursuit.

Jamie turned towards Robin. But his friend hadn't seen the lights. He was looking at a pair of lights that were much closer. Torch lights.

Akela was furious. His voice shook as he shouted at Robin. 'Badgers! You left camp, in the middle of the night, to look at BADGERS?'

Jamie was amazed at how quickly Robin had thought up that one, but he couldn't let his friend take the blame.

'It was my idea, Akela. I knew there was a sett here. I made Robin come with me.'

'How dare you! You know the rules. You're not allowed to leave the camp during the *day* without permission. But to sneak off at night – do you have any idea at all what could have happened to you?'

'No, sir. Sorry, sir.'

'Sorry won't do, Jamie. It's home for both of you. In disgrace. This is the last Cub camp you'll ever attend. I'll see to that.'

Both boys were bundled in blankets and carried back to the camp. Akela's wife stood at the edge of the ring of tents. Her face broke into a relieved smile when she saw the boys, though she quickly damped it and tried to look as cross as her husband. She didn't say anything, though, and gave each boy a quick hug as Akela and his companion set them down close to the dying embers of the campfire.

'They were watching *badgers*,' Akela said, his voice still registering furious amazement.

'Warm clothes and cocoa first. Explanations later,' said Akela's wife firmly. The boys were shepherded into their tent and made to change into fresh tracksuits. The rest of the six were awake – it was David Ross who had first reported the boys' absence to Akela – but nobody was allowed to ask any questions. Robin and Jamie had to spend what remained of the night in Akela's tent, isolated from all the other Cubs until their parents could collect them in the morning.

But in the morning it was not their

parents who came to collect them, but an ambulance. When she got up to supervise the Cubs' breakfast, Akela's wife noticed that Jamie was shivering. As she bent to cover him up, her hand brushed his cheek. It was blazing hot. Both boys had a high fever, and when she tried to wake them, neither Jamie nor Robin stirred.

Chapter 12

For two weeks Jamie and Robin lay in an isolation ward in Heath Road Hospital. They regained consciousness after twenty-four hours, but the fever did not leave them until the sixth day. Both boys had fantastic nightmares, when they cried out and threshed about, drawing their legs up close to their bodies as if afraid their feet might be torn from them.

It was a virus, the doctors said. They did all sorts of tests, even calling in an expert in tropical medicine, but the illness did not resemble any known disease. The fever was straightforward enough, so was the sweating and headache, but no doctor, not even the eminent specialist from Great Ormond

Street, could explain the strange rash. Each boy had it in only one area, on the right leg between ankle and knee. When questioned, neither boy could explain how the rash came to be there. They said they hadn't eaten anything in the forest – no berries, fruits or plants. They knew better than that. Nothing had stung or bitten them. It was a mystery to the medical profession. So they did what they often do – they called it a virus, and were as relieved as were the boys' parents when the illness started to recede.

Both sets of parents had been at the hospital every day. Robin's mum slept in a little room just off the ward, and Mr Mackenzie was given a camp bed next to his son. In the beginning, until the doctors judged the danger was past, they had to put on gowns and masks when they visited Jamie and Robin, and all the boys could see were anxious eyes.

On Saturday Mrs Mackenzie came into the ward with two bulging carrier bags, each filled with *Eagle* and *Tiger* comics and games books.

'Don't tell me, Mum,' said Jamie, 'you've been to a jumble sale!'

'Only to buy these,' said his mother. 'It wasn't the same without you. You're going to have to hurry up and come home.'

Jamie agreed with her. He couldn't wait to get home. He had to get the omniglot back. He just prayed it was still in the hollow tree. What if the slimebags had found it when they had pulled him and Robin out? What if they had returned to Tolly's Hollow and found it later. He had to know!

Once or twice he thought of telling his parents the whole story. But he couldn't. Not yet. They would only inform the authorities and Jamie felt sure that would be the end of it as far as he was concerned. He'd never see the omniglot again. The peace conference would go ahead without it, and there might never be an end to war in the galaxy of Murr. So Jamie made a bargain with himself. He'd give it a month. If he hadn't been able to meet up with the Bdrl and return the omniglot by the time school started again in September, he'd tell his father the whole story.

'And what if the omniglot isn't there when you go back?' Robin asked.

'That,' said Jamie, 'is something I don't want to think about. I wish they would let us go home!'

But another week was to go by before Jamie got his wish, and for Robin, whose leg obstinately refused to improve, it would be even longer.

As soon as general visitors were allowed, Akela came, bringing with him a big card signed by all the Cubs and Scouts.

'I've had a talk with the Commissioner about your little exploit,' he said, pulling up a chair between the two beds, 'and we've decided not to expel you from Cubs. There will have to be some sort of punishment – when you are well enough we want you to clean up the garden around the Cub hut – but in general we feel you've suffered enough for what you did. You'll never wander off alone like that again, will you?'

'No,' chorused Robin and Jamie with matching grins.

'Cub's honour?'

'Cub's honour.'

August the second was Jamie's tenth birthday. The nurses made a big fuss of him. Cards were strung on streamers above his bed, and in the afternoon there was a special birthday tea in the children's playroom. Several of his friends popped in during visiting hours, and Allister brought Jamie a book about Scouting, 'seeing as they're going to let you stay'.

Mr and Mrs Mackenzie trooped in with Cameron and Alice. Jamie was pleased to see the tiddlers again. He was surprised at how much he had missed them. Cameron brought him a book about karate and Alice gave him a football.

Jamie threw it to Robin, who returned it so neatly that Jamie was caught off balance and failed to catch it. There was a shattering sound and a bottle of squash crashed to the floor.

'Anyone can see you're getting better,' said Mum.

Jamie saved his parents' present till last. It was a long thin parcel, like a skinny sausage. Could it be a telescope? Surely not.

He'd been given a pair of binoculars on his last birthday instead of a telescope because they were easier to hold steady.

'Go on. Open it!' urged Dad. 'It isn't your last present. There are more waiting at home from Granny and Grandad.'

Jamie opened it. It wasn't a telescope. It was a bicycle pump.

'There's a new Raleigh waiting in the garage,' said Mrs Mackenzie. 'We thought of bringing it in, but we didn't think they would let you ride it in the corridors. Here's the brochure, though.'

From her handbag she produced a brightly coloured leaflet. Robin jumped out of bed to look at it with Jamie.

'A Raleigh six-speed. You lucky scab!'

'When am I going to get a chance to ride it?'

'That's the other good news. You can come home tomorrow!' said Mr Mackenzie.

'But no long rides for at least a week,' said Jamie's mother firmly. 'You can go as far as the corner shop but no further until you are quite fit again.'

Jamie's heart sank. Time was running out. Would he ever get the omniglot back?

Chapter 13

Mrs Mackenzie stuck to her guns. It was a week before she would let Jamie out of her sight. It didn't matter how many times he protested he felt fine – the corner shop was the limit.

The time passed slowly. Most days they went swimming in Bambridge and then visited Robin in hospital. Jamie felt bad about Rob. He imagined his friend would be jealous that he, Jamie, had got out first. But Robin didn't seem to mind. Years later he admitted to Jamie that he was glad of an excuse not to go back to Tolly's Hollow. The thought of it, and what had happened there, still made his blood run cold.

Allister and David came over several

times with new computer games – Mork's Maze, Globots and Tyrant's Tomb – but somehow they didn't hold Jamie's interest the way they would normally have done. All he could think about was the omniglot.

Night after night he lay awake, wondering how on earth he could contact the Bdrl. Every night he listened for the high-pitched sound. Every night he scanned the sky for yellow lights (he had no wish to see a blue one), but the nights were silent and the skies a screen on which only the stars could be seen.

And then, one night, in that drifting time between wakefulness and sleep, he remembered the slimebag's remark: 'We have two lunars before the conference.'

Lunar meant something to do with the moon. There had been a full moon each time he had seen the spaceships. Did this mean the travellers from Murr could only land on Earth when the moon was full? Jamie slid out of his bunk, found his torch and diary, and turned feverishly to the month of August. Full moon was on 16 August. It was 10 August now. He had six days. Six days to find the omniglot – if it was still in Tolly's Hollow – and figure out a way of contacting the Bdrl. If his guess about the full moon was correct. There were a lot of ifs, but ifs were all he had to go on right now.

Two days later Jamie woke to brilliant sunshine. Cameron and Alice were already up, scrapping over whether to watch He-Man or Transformers on the video.

'You'll watch neither,' Mrs Mackenzie bellowed from her bed. 'Don't you know it is six-thirty in the morning? Get back to bed this minute!'

But it was no good and she knew it. Once the tiddlers were awake there wasn't much more hope of sleep for anyone. Angus would soon be off to work, anyway.

'Come on, then, we'll have a day out,' she said. 'We'll go to the beach at Southwold.'

Here was the chance Jamie had been waiting for. 'Do you mind if I don't come, Mum?' he asked.

'Why not? Aren't you feeling well?'

'It's not that, Mum, but I'd really like a little spin on my new bike. Not far. Just to test it out properly.'

Mrs Mackenzie gave in. 'Okay, I'll make you up a packed lunch when I do ours. But you mustn't tire yourself out – and mind you ride carefully.'

Cameron and Alice went off with Mrs Mackenzie at nine o'clock and Jamie had the house to himself. It was great. He waited a quarter of an hour – his Mum had a habit of coming back for things she'd forgotten and he didn't want her to see him heading out of town. There was only one road to Cranford Forest and if he was seen turning into it there might be some awkward questions asked.

It was a glorious morning. Jamie rode steadily along, the sun beating down on his bike, the new machine going like a bird. It felt good to be wheeling along again. The hedgerows crowded the narrow lane, making borders of dense and tangled green. In the fields beyond, some farmers had already begun the harvest and wheels of hay stood on end like spare tyres for giant tractors.

Cranford Forest looked different by daylight. The sun shafted through the pines and made lacy patterns on the forest floor. The main picnic area was crowded. Jamie could see camper vans and cars parked under the trees. Smoke from barbecues was already wreathing upwards into the clear blue sky.

Jamie had been afraid that the terror he had felt when last in the forest would be waiting for him, but the sunshine seemed to act as an anaesthetic. He still felt lighthearted as he left the main road and cycled up the track to Cranford Lodge. Not even Tolly's Hollow could shake his mood and he felt suddenly certain that everything was going to be all right.

For a second Jamie could not find the hollow tree. Everything looked different somehow. But then he spied the cleft in the trunk through which he and Robin had watched the spaceship land. The entrance was still there; it had only been hidden by undergrowth.

Jamie ducked inside. It was darker here and a faint odour lingered in the air, a dank, dead smell. Jamie quickly felt about for the hole into which he had stuffed the little red box.

It was still there.

Jamie whistled as he rode back to Grant-well. He'd made good time. It was only one o'clock now. He cycled past the house. Good, Mum wasn't back yet.

Now to lay a false trail. He didn't want to have to lie to his mother, and she had never actually said he shouldn't go to Cranford Forest, but somehow he felt it would be better all round if he mentioned a trip to some other destination.

So he spun off on the road to Marshmere. His RSPB card allowed him free entry to the bird sanctuary and he ate his lunch at one of the benches overlooking the beach. Martin Rogers, the warden, joined him and they had a long chat about avocets and other waders. Jamie would have plenty to tell the family when he got home. He decided to buy a bag of fudge for everyone to share, partly because he felt grateful to Mum and the tiddlers for letting him go off alone, and partly to quieten his conscience.

There was a calendar next to the till in the little kiosk. The date was 12 August. Only four days left.

Chapter 14

'I think I might take you to the pictures tonight, Jamie,' beamed his father. 'It's about time you had a treat and they're showing the latest Henton Grant at the cinema in Appleton.'

Jamie was very tempted. The Henton Grant pictures were great and nights out with his dad, just the two of them, were a rare treat, but on this night of all nights he just had to stay home.

'Dad, I'd love to see the film, but could we go another night? I've been on the beach all afternoon and I'm feeling terribly sleepy.'

'I've been on the beach all afternoon too and *I'm* not tired,' said Cameron. Jamie could have kicked him.

'You are not getting over an illness,' Mrs Mackenzie rushed to Jamie's defence. 'You go to bed early, dear. You and Dad can easily go to the pictures another night.'

At eight o'clock Jamie said goodnight to his parents and went up to bed. Cameron was sprawled on his back. He'd thrown the duvet on the floor and covered himself with a sheet instead. It was a very hot night.

Jamie thought about going to bed fully dressed – just in case the summons came – but Mum always looked in on the children on her way to bed and would be bound to notice. In the end he settled for putting on a pair of shorts and a T-shirt under his pyjamas. He'd left his trainers downstairs in the hall. His torch was next to his bunk and the omniglot was under his pillow. Now all he had to do was wait.

Half-past ten came. Jamie hoped his parents wouldn't be too late coming to bed. Dad was playing golf in the morning and Mum was always shattered in the school holidays so there was every chance they would be up soon. At ten to eleven he heard them locking the doors. Mrs Mackenzie came into the boys' bedroom and Jamie heard her putting the duvet back on Cameron's bunk. Jamie lay very quietly. She touched his cheek, briefly, and was gone.

Midnight. Jamie felt as though his ears were out on stalks, he was straining so hard to hear the high-pitched sound. But no sound came. All he could hear was Cameron snuffling in his sleep and the occasional hoot of an owl outside. Through the window he could see the full moon, staring at him as though surprised to find him still awake.

The church clock struck one. Jamie had a sudden alarming thought. What if the omniglot had been damaged during its time in the tree? What if it no longer worked and the Bdrl knew this and had given up and gone home?

He switched on his radio, very quietly, and fiddled with the short-wave knob until he picked up a foreign station. His hand crept under the pillow and traced the shape on the lid of the little red box. The unfamiliar words became a book review. The omniglot still worked.

By now Jamie could hardly keep his eyes open. He tried doing mathematics in his head; made a mental list of all the computer tapes he owned; attempted to make up a limerick beginning 'From Grantwell there came a young girl ...' But eventually all these devices failed, and he fell asleep.

Jamie dreamed. He was lying on Southwold beach and the sun was beating down upon the back of his head. He moved into the shade but still he could not escape the searing sun. He had never known it so hot. He woke up, unsure of his surroundings for a moment. The beach was gone, of course, but the heat remained. He felt his pillow. It was warm, like Mum's bed when the electric blanket had been on for a while.

He moved the pillow – and almost cried out in surprise. The omniglot was glowing. It was no longer a dull red, but had changed to a brilliant fluorescent pink. Carefully, Jamie reached out his hand and touched the box, half expecting to burn his fingers. But it was not unpleasantly hot, just warm, and he found he could pick it up quite easily.

What could it mean? He listened intently,

but there was still no sound to break the stillness of the night. Jamie slid out of his bunk, going off the end rather than risking waking Cameron by using the ladder. With his torch in one hand and the omniglot in the other, he crept downstairs, and, pausing only to take off his pyjamas and slip on his trainers, he went out into the garden.

The sky had that velvety softness that comes just before dawn, but it held no flashing lights of any colour. The omniglot seemed to be getting warmer. On impulse, Jamie flipped it open. The dial inside shone with the same fluorescent light that illuminated the lid. Jamie didn't need the torch to see the strange markings on the outside of the circle – they glowed, almost seeming to pulsate in the darkness.

Something else was different, too. The needle, which Jamie had thought rusted solid, was now moving. It flickered back and forth, back and forth, like the tongue of a snake. The dial looked vaguely familiar. Jamie felt sure he should recognize it. He had seen something like it before. And then suddenly he knew what it was. The round dial, the exactly spaced markings, the needle – it was a compass!

The needle steadied. It was pointing to the uppermost marker. North then. It wanted him to go north towards Marshmere. It would be light in about an hour. The family was unlikely to stir before then. Jamie wrote a quick note to his mum and dad, telling them he'd gone for an early-morning ride, and then, closing the front door very quietly, he slipped out to the shed to collect his bike.

The needle on the dial still pointed north. The omniglot was cooler now, though its colour was no less bright. It had another quality Jamie had not discovered before – it was magnetic. As Jamie was wondering how he could cycle and consult the dial at the same time, the omniglot was tugged from his hand and fixed itself securely to the chromium-plated steel handlebars. He was on the trail of the Bdrl at last.

Chapter 15

After a couple of miles, the needle changed direction. It was pointing east now, towards the sea. Jamie took the next road to the right, not much more than a lane. It took him past Salters Farm. There was a light on in the milking shed and an orderly queue of patient cows, all waiting to go into their stalls. A dog started to bark and Jamie rode on as fast as he could. He could do without any hold-ups now.

Still the needle pointed to the sea. Jamie topped a rise and almost fell off his bike when the needle did an abrupt about turn. It was now pointing due south. There was no road, not even a footpath, but Jamie did see a farm gate in the half-light of the early morning. Beyond it there was a very faint track.

Jamie parked his bike, tucking it into the hedge so that it would be invisible from the lane, and set off on foot, the omniglot showing the way. He crossed one field, then another, and just as he was beginning to give up hope of ever meeting the Bdrl, she was there.

A small silvery figure, she looked like an older version of his sister Alice, and not at all like the fearsomely horrible form of the slimebag. She (Jamie was sure it was a girl) was smaller than Jamie and differently proportioned.

Her legs seemed unusually long, her body especially slender. Her face, which was turned towards Jamie with a look of welcome, was the most beautiful he had ever seen. It didn't look like an earthly face, although it had the same features. There was something about the arrangement of eyes, nose and lips that was subtly different and yet very lovely.

She spoke, a liquid sound, like the song of a nightingale. Jamie closed the lid of the omniglot and his fingers touched the linked stars. He slid the panel to one side and inserted the earplugs in his ears.

'You have come, Jamie. I knew you would.'

Her use of his name startled Jamie and for a moment he felt nervous.

'Don't be afraid. We would never harm you. We owe you everything.'

Jamie held out the omniglot.

'No. Keep it a moment, then we can talk. I am Talya. Will you come into my spaceship?'

Jamie looked around. He couldn't see anything that looked even remotely like a spaceship.

'You won't see it. It's shielded. We couldn't risk detection.'

She led the way across the field and suddenly stopped short, her arm outstretched, her hand flat, as though pressed against an unseen surface. Jamie copied her action and found himself touching a cold, very faintly pitted surface. The girl was climbing steps. It was odd to see her treading the air, but Jamie followed and found himself doing the same.

She moved forward. Jamie followed – and banged his head.

'Oh, I'm sorry. I forgot you were taller
than I.'

'That's okay.'

Jamie took a step towards her and stopped in amazement. He was in his own bedroom. The bunks – both empty – were
neatly made, the bookshelf tidy in the corner. His television set sat on the desk along-
side his computer. Tapes lay in an untidy
pile, just as they always did.

'What on earth!'

She moved to his side. 'You are not
pleased. I am so sorry. It was my idea. I
thought you would feel more comfortable if
the surroundings were familiar.'

'I'm not angry, only startled. You don't
expect to find your own bedroom in a spaceship.'

'It's just an illusion.'

'How did you know what my room looked
like?'

'We scanned your home.'

'You've been spying on me?' Jamie felt
angry.

'No. Not until tonight. We didn't even
know where you lived until a short while

ago, when we activated the omniglot.'

'Why did you do that? Why didn't you just call me with the high-pitched sound, like you did last time?'

Talya looked puzzled. 'Sound? We don't use sound signals.' Her face cleared, and then became grave. 'It must have been the Fwe. They have an audio tracking device. But it uses a very high frequency. Few humans can detect it. You must have unusually acute hearing.'

Jamie smiled. So *that* was why he had been the only one to hear the sound!

He told Talya about his meeting with the Fwe. When he described them as slimebags she chuckled, but looked alarmed when he told the rest of the story.

'It was I who startled them in the clearing. I never knew they had prisoners, though. They must have left you and come chasing me. You don't know how lucky you were not to be killed. I had been tracking them ever since Osk was murdered.'

'Osk?'

'Oh, dear, I think I had better tell you everything. But first, shall I change this room? I don't think you are truly comfortable.'

'I'd rather see it as it usually is.'

Talya touched a badge on her chest and Jamie's bedroom disappeared, much to his relief. He had found it decidedly creepy. In its place was a clinical-looking room, rather like the control centre of a power plant Jamie had once visited. There were banks of equipment and various screens. Against the walls were moulded seats, their colour like nothing Jamie had ever seen on earth, and each bearing the marking Jamie now recognized as Bdrl.

Watching the transformation of the room Jamie had a sudden and not very pleasant thought.

'If you can create an illusion of a place, what about a person?'

Talya looked puzzled for a moment and then giggled.

'You mean me? Do you think I am an illusion and underneath is a ghastly monster?'

Jamie grinned weakly.

'Sorry to disappoint you, but this is the real me.'

Jamie felt very relieved. Talya motioned him to sit down.

'As you know, our galaxy, Murr, has been at war for many meganni. My generation know nothing else. We have had enough. Not only the young people of my planet but the young of every world in the galaxy (with the possible exception of the Fwe). There is a growing peace movement and we have organized an intergalactic convention to discuss the subject. We had real hope of peace when one of our scientists developed a device that could enable all the delegates to understand one another.'

'The omniglot.'

'Precisely. It is quite a simple device really, and we had hopes of producing it in bulk so that one day every inhabitant of Murr would have one. This would, of course, be no guarantee of peace, but we felt that if people would only talk and understand each other, there would be a beginning.

'The Fwe wanted us stopped. You know why. That was one of the reasons we brought the prototype to your planet for testing. Earth is an ideal testing

114

ground – you too have many peoples, much distrust and many wars. And your planet is a long way from Murr – far enough, we thought, to escape the Fwe.'

'But you were wrong.'

'As you found out. Yes. Fwe spies traced our scientist. His name was Osk, a brave and clever man. When he realized he had been followed it was too late for him to escape. He hid the omniglot in some old boxes outside a wooden building.'

The church hall. Of course! So that was how the box had got into the jumble sale, Jamie thought excitedly.

Talya went on: 'Osk led the Fwe a dance, but they tracked him and four days later his spaceship crashed in a forest near here, the same forest where you encountered the slimebags, as you called them.'

'I think I saw the spot where he crashed.' Jamie told Talya about the outing with his parents, when he had seen the star symbol in the scorched earth.

'That would be the place. Our spaceships are designed to vaporize if they crash so that they do not leave any evidence behind for alien civilizations. The last thing to go is the metal symbol on the underbelly. It always leaves a faint imprint, like a brand, in the soil.'

'Then what happened?'

'When Osk disappeared, and with him the prototype, there was panic on my planet as there was no time to manufacture another omniglot before the conference. I was sent to investigate. We established that the omniglot was still operational – it emits a faint signal – but we had a job tracking you down. Just when we thought we had located you the signal moved far away.'

'That must have been when we went to France.'

'Oh. Well, matters were not helped by the fact that we can only actually land on Earth when your satellite is fully visible.'

'Full moon. I guessed that.'

'Eventually we had to risk activating the omniglot. It was a risk because the Fwe could have found you as easily as we did, but we had no option. Time is running out.'

'Where are the Fwe now?'

Talya moved to a monitoring screen.

116

'Near. Too near. They must have picked up the signal. You must go now.'

She put out her hand for the omniglot. 'Jamie, my people thank you. Your courage may have saved a galaxy. We will remember you always.'

There was nothing else to say. Jamie regretfully returned the earplugs to their nest and handed the omiglot to Talya.

Seconds later he was standing at the edge of the field, alone. Momentarily the spaceship became visible, a glorious gleaming silver disc bathed in golden-yellow light. And then there was just the shimmering air.

Chapter 16

Four years had passed. Jamie and Robin were at the high school now. There had been no more lights over Suffolk, no more strange sounds in the night. There were days when both boys doubted the events of that odd summer had ever taken place, and had it not been for a dull silvery scar that each boy bore on his ankle, they might have begun to feel it had been a dream – or a nightmare.

Jamie still found it easy to learn foreign languages. The omniglot seemed to have attuned his own ears somehow and he was top of the class in both French and German. Sometimes, late at night, he would lie awake thinking about a girl with hair like silver and a voice like music, a girl he had met on a dewy morning four years before. He wished he knew whether she had succeeded in making her dream of peace a reality.

And then, one night when the moon was full, Jamie heard once again the piercing high-pitched sound that had come to him that long hot summer.

He sat up in bed – he had his own room now – and looked out of the window. Two lights danced in the sky, one yellow, one blue. Briefly they passed in front of his window, describing an arc in the sky, and then, quite suddenly, they were gone.

Jamie felt bereft, as though something he treasured was lost to him for ever. He opened the window to search the sky for those elusive lights – and drew in his breath with a gasp.

Something was lying on the windowsill. Something familiar. A small box, dark red in colour, with linked stars on the lid.

Jamie's hands shook as he opened the box. It looked as it had on that faraway day when he had brought it home from the jumble sale.

The needle on the dial was fixed and motionless, the figures around the circle dull.

He slid the panel on the lid aside. The compartment was still there, the earplugs still in place. But this time there were three of them. In addition to the pair of white plugs there was a small blue capsule.

What was it for?

Jamie slipped the blue plug into his ear. Immediately he heard it, a voice like liquid music, sweetly murmuring in his head: 'It's me, Jamie. Talya. After all this time! I bet you had begun to think you would never hear the end of the story.

'I hated saying goodbye to you, but the Fwe were coming and they very nearly caught me. How I escaped them I shall never know. But I did. And the peace conference went ahead. It was a great success. All the sessions went on twice as long as they should have – the delegates just couldn't stop talking!

'Peace didn't come overnight. There are still some war-torn areas. But for the first time within Murr, there is real hope for the future.

'And all this is largely thanks to you. That's why I have been able to pay a brief visit to Earth, to bring you the original omniglot. It will only work while our spaceships are in the vicinity to act as transmitters, so it won't be much use to you, but we thought you would like to have it to remember us by.

'You wouldn't recognize the omniglot now. It has been miniaturized and made even easier to use. The latest ones can even play back recorded messages like the one you are listening to. Every household in the galaxy has one now and we hope the day will soon come when we can issue one to every adult and every child.

'And you'll never guess who are manufacturing them. Yes. The Fwe! It seemed quite logical really. They had all the engineering skill and the technology. The machinery so long used to make weapons for war proved surprisingly simple to adapt for instruments of peace.

'Today the Fwe are the most enthusiastic ambassadors for peace in our galaxy. They are still motivated by greed, of course, but even that is changing as they learn more about other planets and about themselves.

'It is a pity you do not have the omniglot on Earth, Jamie. One day you will have the necessary technology. One day soon. Our scientists estimate that within the next five years your planet will be ready for the omniglot. And when it is, we will help you, Jamie, to be its "inventor".

'This is not goodbye, Jamie. We shall meet again.'